In memory of my father, Alexander Munro King. 1918 – 2000

Tiptoe softly as you go

bears lie sleeping under snow...

AUTHOR'S NOTE

The Bear and its wilderness habitat are under constant threat: they need our protection. Deborah King's story captures the hearts and dreams of any child who curls up each night with a much loved bear. This magical journey into their secret world is evoked in lyrical verse and atmospheric illustrations. We view the bears through the eyes of a little girl and contrast her world with theirs, yet the perspective on bear life remains a realistic one.

Throughout the ages, Bears have inspired us. They have provided us with many loveable characters and enriched children's literature, music and film. Now, their future is uncertain and it is time for us to give something back. One such organisation working to protect their forest habitat in South East Alaska is SEACC, a member of the Alaskan Rainforest Foundation. They run education programmes working both at grassroots level and with resource management agencies and the U.S. Congress, to ensure a future for the people, the Tongass Forest and all its wildlife. If you would like to learn more about the Bear's world and how the forest is managed, you can write to them at: SEACC, 419 6th St. #328, Juneau. Alaska 99801, U.S.A. Email: info@seacc.org. Homepage: http://www.juneau.com/seacc/

And if you would like to know more about 'The Fortress of the Bears', the island in the Tongass where Deborah King made her journey, you can write to: Friends of Admiralty Island, PO Box 204, Angoon, Alaska 99820. For information on Bears on other continents contact: WWF, Panda House, Weyside Park, Godalming, Surrey, GU7 1XR

ACKNOWLEDGEMENTS:
I would especially like to thank wilderness guide, David Ford who organised my trip to Alaska and whose enterprise, commitment and support turned a lifelong dream into reality.
Thanks also to K.J and Peggy Metcalf, JoAnn George in Angoon; Bart Koehler, Rob and Corin Bosworth in Juneau; Kimmer Ford, Dick Griffith in Anchorage and Lemesurier Isle, and Paul Barnes in Gustavus for making me so welcome. Closer to home, thanks to Lauren Churchill, Margaret Dray, George Harrison and most especially, Dave and Madi Precious.

1 3 5 7 9 10 8 6 4 2   First published in Great Britain by HarperCollins Publishers Ltd in 2000
ISBN: 0 00 198323 7   Text and illustration copyright © Deborah King 2000
The Harpercollins website address is www.fireandwater.com
Printed and bound in Singapore.

Bear's Dream

DEBORAH KING

Collins

An imprint of HarperCollinsPublishers

When the land is white with snow,
the city clean and bright
and quiet,
beyond the hills
there is a forest,
and further still,
a mountain at the top of the world.

And somewhere up there
in the mountain caves,
the dark dens,
on beds of woody bark,
bears are sleeping
without a sound.
Nothing stirs
underground,
not a whisper
all winter long.

All around
there are no flowers
and no bird-song.
I play outside,
make a snowman.
I dance *quick, quick slow…*
round and round
my footprints go.
I slip and slide
throw snowballs until my fingers freeze.
And all the while
sleepy bears keep nice and warm,
buried under days and days
of deepening snow.

I walk on tiptoe.
Whispering softly as I go,
"Bears lie sleeping under snow."
What do they eat
or drink
or think about
in their silent midnight world?
"All they need is sleep," says grandpa.
"You see, the bears are dreaming."

…And as I hold my old bear tight
and lights go out,
I wonder...
"Will their dreams come true?"

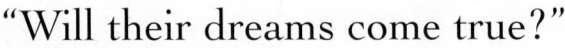

And on the cruellest, coldest winter nights
some dreams do…
A bear gives birth.
Twins are born
inside the earth
on midwinter's darkest night.

But no one knows.
No one will find them sleeping under snow.
Not until the Northern Lights
beam violet, green and gold,
and skies burn bright
and flowers grow
and birds sing
will bears bring cubs out into the sun
to begin their spring dance…

…to step out
one by one
in melting snow,
sink perfect pawprints
quick quick slow
as down and down they go
to lush green valleys
and ancient woodlands
far below,
by flowing stream
and lake
and waterfall.
Bears big and small
roll and play,
graze meadow flowers, rush and sedge
all making for the water's edge,
all going to the sea,
like me.

But some bears

watch us from behind bars.

We feed them through the winter,

so they stay awake

for you and me

But we break their hearts

and take away their dream.

They will never see
trees tall enough
to touch the moon,
or hear the loon sing
across the lake,
where wild bears take siestas
under canopies of green
and eagles fly the blue sky
in between
and ravens call,
and bears are listening,
but they're nowhere to be seen.
That's where a bear should be,
far away from you and me
unreachable,
ble,

I dance and sing a summer song.
I clap my hands
one..two..three..
"Where are you, Bear?
Hey, Bear, it's me!"
But the bears are busy.
They're going fishing
just like me.

It's hot.
I paddle like a bear.
I search for crabs in shallow pools,
swim and splash,
keep nice and cool
and shake my long wet hair
…just like a bear.

While far away
bears chase much bigger dreams,
fishing in the salmon streams.

On other days
they dig for grubs,
crunching beetles
munching bugs,
picking rosehips,
nuts and berries,
scooping strawberries
off the forest floor,
eating
until they can eat no more…

…until the rains come
and the wind blows cold from the north
and the mists cloud the sun,
and the leaves start to fall
one by one.
Then all the bears will be gone,
up through the trees
to the mountain at the top of the world.

No one knows where they are,
But I do.
And sometimes, on winter nights
when I curl up tight with my old bear,
from far beyond the hills
I can hear their heartbeats,
bears dreaming sweet dreams
for me and you,
softly
under snow.

THE LAND OF THE BROWN BEAR

BEAR'S DREAM came about during a visit I made to Alaska in the summer of 1998. I made an unforgettable journey into a bear's world, back-packing the forest trails, and kayaking the lake chain running down to the salmon creeks and rocky shores off Admiralty Island, S.E Alaska. This island is also known as 'Kootznoowoo' in honour of the native people, the Tlingit who fought to protect it, achieving designated wilderness status in 1980 to become the largest area of protected old growth temperate rain forest in the world.

Here, a fragile balance between man and nature has been preserved. This is a unique place where wildlife outnumbers humans and where people, (i.e. hunters, miners, scientists, tourists) are carefully managed to give the bears rights of way. Bears need this protection. Even amongst their own kind, they are loners seeking solitude.

Once Brown Bears were widespread across three continents and had no natural enemies. Now it seems they exist only with our permission. In our need for timber, oil and minerals, we destroy vast irreplaceable tracts of ancient forest, and build roads deeper and deeper into wilderness areas. This threat to the bear is further compounded by the activities of trophy hunters, poachers, and tourists. And unfortunately, some bears have come to associate people with garbage dumps and easy pickings, leading to serious conflict and ultimately, danger for the bears.

But our age-old fear of the bear is largely based on ignorance. Unless threatened, bears are seldom dangerous. When observed in areas previously untouched by man, bears have proved themselves to be curious and trusting creatures. Unlike us, they are quietly accepting of our presence, showing no fear or aggression.

For centuries, the Native people have shared the land with the bears. They both fear and respect them, admiring them for their power and intelligence, and in the past have named many of their chiefs and elders, mountains and valleys in their honour. When they killed a bear, they would ask its forgiveness. When travelling through the forest, they talked to the bears so as not to startle them, thereby ensuring their own safety, (a technique guides now adopt as routine when moving through bear country).

They believe the bear to have human qualities, here to remind us of the dark, secret side of ourselves. After all, it walks on the heels and soles of its feet and can stand up like us, using its paws and long curved claws like hands and fingers. More remarkable, it can endure a winter of solitary confinement, without food or drink, in complete darkness for as long as six months or more. Unlike other hibernators, the bear is unique in that it stays warm, easily aroused in times of danger. Equally incredible, the mother bear gives birth to such tiny cubs, she can often lie undisturbed by the event and experience the raising of her young in her sleep.

In Native American tradition, the big sleep of the bears is an important part of nature's cycle. It is seen as an opportunity for deep thought and contemplation and a time of healing. As the earth rests to renew her strength, so the bears retreat to their dens, to wake from their winter of dreaming empowered with new found knowledge and wisdom, to re-emerge at sunrise, harbingers of spring to the northern world.

We should listen to the ancient peoples and learn to understand the needs of the bear. We should endeavour to protect their forests, leave wilderness areas untouched and unexplored, and above all…..LEAVE ROOM FOR BEARS.